W9-APR-154

TERRORIST:
GAVRILO PRINCIP, THE ASSASSIN
WHO IGNITED WORLD WAR I

TERRORIST.

GAVRILO PRINCIP, THE ASSASSIN WHO IGNITED WORLD WAR I

HENRIK REHR

GRAPHIC UNIVERSE™ · MINNEAPOLIS

THE AUTHOR THANKS ALLAN HAVERHOLM, PAW MATHIASEN, KRISTIAN REHR, BOB MECOY, ALAIN DAVID AND THE FRIENDLY TEAM AT THE NEW YORK PUBLIC LIBRARY, WITHOUT WHOM THIS BOOK WOULD NOT HAVE HAPPENED.

STORY AND ART BY HENRIK REHR

FIRST AMERICAN EDITION PUBLISHED IN 2015 BY GRAPHIC UNIVERSE™.
PUBLISHED BY ARRANGEMENT WITH FUTUROPOLIS.

GAVRILO PRINCIP: L'HOMME QUI CHANGEA LE SIÈCLE BY HENRIK REHR
COPYRIGHT © FUTUROPOLIS, PARIS, 2014
COPYRIGHT © 2015 BY LERNER PUBLISHING GROUP, INC., FOR THE US EDITION

GRAPHIC UNIVERSE™ IS A TRADEMARK OF LERNER PUBLISHING GROUP, INC.

ALL US RIGHTS RESERVED. NO PART OF THIS BOOK MAY BE REPRODUCED, STORED IN A RETRIEVAL SYSTEM, OR TRANSMITTED IN ANY FORM OR BY ANY MEANS—ELECTRONIC, MECHANICAL, PHOTOCOPYING, RECORDING, OR OTHERWISE—WITHOUT THE PRIOR WRITTEN PERMISSION OF LERNER PUBLISHING GROUP, INC., EXCEPT FOR THE INCLUSION OF BRIEF QUOTATIONS IN AN ACKNOWLEDGED REVIEW.

GRAPHIC UNIVERSE™
A DIVISION OF LERNER PUBLISHING GROUP, INC.
241 FIRST AVENUE NORTH
MINNEAPOLIS, MN 55401 USA

FOR READING LEVELS AND MORE INFORMATION, LOOK UP THIS TITLE AT WWW.LERNERBOOKS.COM.

LIBRARY OF CONGRESS CATALOGING-IN-PUBLICATION DATA

REHR, HENRIK.
      [GAVRILO PRINCIP, L'HOMME QUI CHANGEA LE SIÈCLE. ENGLISH]
    TERRORIST : GAVRILO PRINCIP, THE ASSASSIN WHO IGNITED WORLD WAR I / WRITTEN AND ILLUSTRATED BY HENRIK REHR. — FIRST AMERICAN EDITION.
        PAGES   CM
    SUMMARY: FICTIONAL ACCOUNT OF THE LIFE OF THE YOUNG SERBIAN TERRORIST, GAVRILO PRINCIP, WHO TOUCHED OFF WORLD WAR I IN 1914 BY ASSASSINATING THE ARCHDUKE FRANZ FERDINAND.
      ISBN 978-1-4677-7279-2 (LIB. BDG. : ALK. PAPER) — ISBN 978-1-4677-7284-6 (PBK.) — ISBN 978-1-4677-7285-3 (EB PDF)
      1. GRAPHIC NOVELS. [1. GRAPHIC NOVELS. 2. PRINCIP, GAVRILO, 1894-1918—FICTION. 3. ASSASSINS—FICTION. 4. SERBS—BOSNIA AND HERCEGOVINA—FICTION. 5. WORLD WAR, 1914-1918—FICTION.] I. TITLE.
    PZ7.7.R45GAV 2015
    741.5'944—DC23
                                                          2014021939

MANUFACTURED IN THE UNITED STATES OF AMERICA
1 — BP — 12/31/14

SARAJEVO, JUNE 28, 1914

BANG

"BEFORE WE PART, I WOULD LIKE TO EXPRESS THE WISH THAT YOU UNDERSTAND US, THAT YOU NOT CONSIDER US CRIMINALS.

"OUR PEOPLE SCREAM, LIVE IN MISERY. THEY HAVE NO SCHOOLS, NO CULTURE. IT HURTS US. WE FELT THE ANGUISH OF OUR PEOPLE.

"WE DIDN'T HATE THE HAPSBURG DYNASTY. YES, I NOURISHED ANARCHISTIC IDEAS, YES, I HATED EVERYTHING, BUT I NEVER IN A SINGLE THOUGHT BORE ILL WILL AGAINST HIS HIGHNESS FRANZ JOSEPH.

"ALTHOUGH PRINCIP ACTS AS THE HERO, ALTHOUGH ALL OF US ACT AS THE HERO, WE'RE NEVERTHELESS VERY SORRY, BECAUSE WE DIDN'T KNOW, IN THE FIRST PLACE, THAT THE LATE FRANZ FERDINAND WAS THE FATHER OF A FAMILY.

"I BEG THAT THE CHILDREN OF THE HEIR APPARENT FORGIVE US AND THAT YOU RENDER WHATEVER VERDICT YOU LIKE.

"WE AREN'T EVILDOERS; WE'RE HONEST PEOPLE, HONORABLE, IDEALISTIC. WE WANTED TO DO GOOD, WE LOVED OUR PEOPLE AND WE WILL DIE FOR OUR IDEAS."

COURT TRANSCRIPT OF STATEMENT BY NEDELJKO ČABRINOVIĆ, SARAJEVO, OCTOBER 23, 1914

"EUROPE TODAY IS A POWDER KEG,
AND THE LEADERS ARE LIKE MEN
SMOKING IN AN ARSENAL...
A SINGLE SPARK WILL SET OFF AN
EXPLOSION THAT WILL CONSUME US ALL...
I CAN'T TELL YOU WHEN THAT EXPLOSION
WILL OCCUR, BUT I CAN TELL YOU WHERE...
SOME DAMNED FOOLISH THING IN THE
BALKANS WILL SET IT OFF."

—OTTO VON BISMARCK,
GERMAN CHANCELLOR, 1862–1890

THE TRUTH IS WRITTEN IN WATER.

THIS IS A TRUE STORY.

ARCHDUKE FRANZ FERDINAND OF HABSBURG WAS BORN ON DECEMBER 18, 1863, THE ELDEST SON OF THE EMPEROR'S BROTHER, KARL LUDWIG.

FRANZ WAS, ON THE WHOLE, AN UNREMARKABLE YOUNG MAN, AN OFFICER AND A GENTLEMAN FOR SURE BUT ALSO YET JUST ANOTHER MALE OCCUPANT OF THE HOUSE OF HAPSBURG.

THAT IS, UNTIL JANUARY 29, 1889, WHEN HIS COUSIN RUDOLF, THE CROWN PRINCE, WENT TO THE HUNTING LODGE IN MAYERLING WITH HIS MISTRESS, MARY VETSERA.

RUDOLF, AT ODDS WITH HIS FATHER, THE EMPEROR, OVER POLITICS AND RUDOLF'S MEMBERSHIP IN THE FREEMASONS, MADE A FATEFUL DECISION.

BANG

SUDDENLY, FRANZ FERDINAND WAS THE HEIR APPARENT TO THE THRONE OF AUSTRIA-HUNGARY.

"KRAJINA'S LIKE A BLOOD-SOAKED RAG.
BLOOD IS OUR FARE AT NOON, BLOOD STILL IN THE EVENING.
ON EVERY LIP THE TASTE OF BLOOD.
NEVER A PEACEFUL DAY, NEVER ANY REST."

—SERBIAN FOLK SONG

THE PRINCIPS WERE ORTHODOX CHRISTIANS LIVING IN THE VILLAGE OBLJAJ IN THE KRAJINA REGION OF WESTERN SERBIA.

FOR GENERATIONS THEY FARMED THE LAND RENTED TO THEM BY THEIR MUSLIM LANDOWNER.

SCHÖNBRUNN PALACE
IN VIENNA

YOU WISHED TO SEE ME, UNCLE?

THE OFFICE OF EMPEROR FRANZ JOSEPH

THIS MATTER WITH THE CHOTEK WOMAN MUST STOP IMMEDIATELY.

HER FAMILY MIGHT BE OF OLD CZECH NOBILITY, BUT SHE'S **FAR** BELOW YOUR STATION.

BREAK OFF THE AFFAIR AND FIND SOME OTHER AMUSEMENT.

YOU'RE DISMISSED.

I SAID...

I HEARD YOU, UNCLE, BUT I LOVE SOPHIE, AND I **MUST** MARRY HER. IT'S NOT ONLY A MATTER OF THE HEART, BUT OF MY LIFE, MY EXISTENCE, AND MY FUTURE.

IF YOU FORCE MY HAND IN THIS, I **SHALL** KILL MYSELF.

YOUR CHILDREN WILL NEVER BE ABLE TO INHERIT THE THRONE.

AS LONG AS THEY ARE SOPHIE'S, WHAT DOES IT MATTER?

ON JULY 1, 1899, FRANZ FERDINAND AND SOPHIE CHOTEK WERE MARRIED IN THE ARCHDUKE'S CASTLE IN BOHEMIA.

IN THE NINETEENTH CENTURY THE OTTOMAN EMPIRE'S HOLD ON THE BALKANS HAD BEGUN TO WEAKEN. WITH THE TREATY OF BERLIN IN 1878, SERBIA, MONTENEGRO, ROMANIA, AND BULGARIA GAINED THEIR INDEPENDENCE AFTER FIVE HUNDRED YEARS OF MUSLIM RULE.

SLOVENIA AND CROATIA CONTINUED TO BE GOVERNED BY AUSTRIA-HUNGARY, WHICH ALSO TOOK CONTROL OF BOSNIA-HERZEGOVINA, ALTHOUGH THE PEOPLE OF THE LATTER STILL TECHNICALLY WERE TURKISH CITIZENS.

INSPIRED BY ITALY'S EXAMPLE, DREAMS OF UNIFICATION OF ALL THE SOUTHERN SLAVS BEGAN TO ARISE IN THE REGION. BY THE TURN OF THE CENTURY, IT WAS OBVIOUS TO BOTH THE TURKS AND THE AUSTRIANS THAT SERBIA WAS A FORCE TO BE RECKONED WITH.

A SERBIAN KNIGHT, MILOŠ OBILIĆ, THEN PRETENDED TO SURRENDER TO THE OTTOMAN SULTAN, MURAD.

MILOŠ INSISTED ON BEING PRESENTED TO MURAD TO OFFER THE TURKS THE SERVICES OF MILOŠ'S TROOPS IN THE BATTLE.

WHEN THE KNIGHT WAS BROUGHT BEFORE THE SULTAN, MILOŠ STABBED HIM WITH A POISONED KNIFE.

MURAD EXPIRED.

STILL, THE SERBIAN ARMY WAS DEFEATED.

PRINCE LAZAR WAS BEHEADED.

IN HIS GRIEF, MURAD'S SON, BEYAZID, ORDERED ALL THE PRISONERS EXECUTED.

THE FIELD OF THE BLACKBIRDS RAN RED WITH OUR PRECIOUS BLOOD.

I'LL TAKE GAVRILO OVER THE MOUNTAINS TO THE RAILWAY STATION NEXT WEEK.

A WISE DECISION. HE HAS NO CHANCE OF MAKING A DECENT LIVING IN THIS GODFORSAKEN VALLEY.

GAVRO, COME HERE.

BE CAREFUL IN THE CITY, BOY. TOWNSPEOPLE ARE VERY DIFFERENT FROM THE GENTLE FOLKS YOU'VE GROWN UP WITH HERE.

AND NEVER, **NEVER** FORGET WHO YOU ARE. SARAJEVO'S FULL OF MUSLIMS, AUSTRIANS, CROATS, WHAT HAVE YOU. BE A SERB ABOVE ALL ELSE.

ALWAYS CARRY THE KRAJINA VALLEY IN YOUR HEART.

ALWAYS.

SARAJEVO.

JOVO!

GOOD TO SEE YOU, LITTLE BROTHER!

A FRIEND OF MINE CHANGED MY MIND ABOUT THE MILITARY SCHOOL. YOU'RE NOT GOING THERE. **AUSTRIANS** WILL BE TEACHING. YOU'D FEEL LIKE A STRANGER, AND YOU DON'T NEED YOUR MIND POISONED BY THEIR IDEAS.

I'VE ENROLLED YOU IN A COMMERCIAL SCHOOL INSTEAD. THERE'S A LOT OF MONEY TO BE MADE IN THE BAZAAR HERE.

UNFORTUNATELY, I DON'T HAVE SPACE FOR YOU AT HOME WITH THE NEW BABY AND EVERYTHING, BUT I'VE GOT YOU A ROOM WITH MRS. ILIČ.

I WAS HOPING TO STAY WITH YOU.

SAY, DID DAD BUY YOU A SUITCASE?

SECOND-HAND.

STILL.

I WAS SENT OFF TO SARAJEVO WITH NOTHING BUT THE CLOTHES ON MY BACK.

FOR MY BOOKS, I GUESS.

MRS. ILIĆ'S A WIDOW AND DECENT ENOUGH, BUT STAY AWAY FROM HER SON, DANILO.

HE CAN'T HOLD A JOB, THE LAZY GOOD-FOR-NOTHING.

LEAVES HIS MOTHER TO DO PEOPLE'S LAUNDRY.

COME TO DINNER ON SATURDAY...AND STAY OUT OF TROUBLE, LITTLE BROTHER.

SEE YOU.

SEE YOU.

LAZY! LAZY?

DO YOU KNOW HOW MUCH MONEY I SPENT ON YOUR SCHOOL? NOT TO MENTION ROOM AND BOARD HERE! AND **THESE** ARE THE GRADES YOU GET?!

THE AUSTRIANS THINK THEIR EMPIRE WILL LAST FOREVER, BUT THEY FORGET **HISTORY!**

THE WORD *SLAVE* DERIVES FROM "SLAVIC," BECAUSE THE ROMANS GOT THE MAJORITY OF THEIR THRALLS FROM AROUND THESE PARTS.

REMEMBER **SPARTACUS!** HE GREW UP IN DALMATIA; WAS TAKEN AS A SLAVE BY THE ROMANS AND EVENTUALLY BECAME A GLADIATOR; DESTINED TO **DIE** FOR THE **AMUSEMENT** OF THE UPPER CLASSES!

BUT SPARTACUS WASN'T ABOUT TO JUST ACCEPT HIS FATE. HE STARTED A **REBELLION** AT THE GLADIATOR SCHOOL AND **SLAUGHTERED** HIS OPPRESSORS.

SOON SLAVES FROM **ALL OVER** THE ITALIAN PENINSULA JOINED IN THE UPRISING.

FOR THREE YEARS THE SLAVE ARMY **HAUNTED** AND **TERRIFIED** THE MIGHTY ROMAN EMPIRE, AND MARK MY WORDS... THE AUSTRIAN EMPIRE WILL BE HAUNTED AND TERRIFIED WHEN **WE** RISE UP TO CAST OFF THEIR INSIDIOUS YOKE! LIKE SPARTACUS'S ARMY, WE SHALL RISE FROM BELOW AND **CRUSH** OUR OPPRESSORS!

THEN AND ONLY **THEN** WILL WE BE ABLE TO UNITE ALL SOUTHERN SLAVS IN A NEW COUNTRY WITH BELGRADE AS ITS CAPITAL!

OKAY, VLADIMIR, ENOUGH GRAND-STANDING FOR TONIGHT. COME DOWN FROM THE CHAIR AND HAVE A DRINK.

I DISAGREE WITH YOU, VLADIMIR! COURAGE AS SUCH DOESN'T EXIST. IT'S ALL A MATTER OF PRESSURES AND REWARDS.

SARAJEVO

FOR INSTANCE, IT WOULD BE **CRAZY** OF ME TO JUMP INTO THE RIVER TONIGHT!

NOT REALLY. YOU DESPERATELY NEED A BATH!

HEE—HEE

WITH ALL THE WATER COMING DOWN FROM THE MOUNTAINS, THERE'S A GOOD CHANCE I MIGHT **DROWN!**

BUT IF I MADE A **BET** WITH YOU TWO, IF I COULD WIN A GOOD DEAL OF MONEY BY RISKING DEATH, I JUST **MAY** JUMP!

I'LL PUT UP MY RENT MONEY FOR THE NEXT THREE MONTHS.

ME TOO.

48

GAVRO! GRAB MY HAND!

...BUT WITHOUT GOD, THERE'S NO MYSTERY IN LIFE! AND NO MORALS!

PEOPLE DON'T NEED A DEITY TO BEHAVE DECENTLY! LOVE, JUSTICE, BEAUTY...ALL THOSE THINGS HAVE VALUE IN THEMSELVES.

WHY DO WE REQUIRE AN OLD SUPERSTITION TO INFUSE OUR EXISTENCE WITH MEANING? GOD'S DEAD AND ALWAYS WAS. THE RULING CLASSES JUST USED OUR FEAR OF HIM TO KEEP US IN OUR PLACE.

STOP IT! I WON'T HEAR THAT KIND OF TALK IN FRONT OF MY KIDS!

BAM

SORRY.

IT'S FOR YOUR OWN SAKE, GAVRO...TALKING LIKE THAT, YOU'LL END UP IN HELL!

I'M A BOSNIAN SERB. I'M ALREADY THERE!

THE GEOPOLITICAL MAP OF EUROPE IN THE EARLY TWENTIETH CENTURY WAS RIDDLED WITH MILITARY ALLIANCES.

SERBIA WAS ALLIED WITH RUSSIA. RUSSIA WAS ALLIED WITH FRANCE, AND FRANCE WAS ALLIED WITH GREAT BRITAIN.

ON THE OTHER SIDE, GERMANY WAS ALLIED WITH AUSTRIA–HUNGARY AND ITALY.

COMBINE THAT WITH A FEVERISH ARMS RACE—FOR EXAMPLE, THE GERMAN AND FRENCH ARMIES DOUBLED IN SIZE BETWEEN 1870 AND 1914—AND YOU HAVE A SITUATION THAT IS RATHER…PRECARIOUS.

THE AUSTRIAN PROCLAMATION OF THE ANNEXATION OF BOSNIA-HERZEGOVINA CAUSED AN UPROAR IN SERBIA.

LARGE DEMONSTRATIONS TOOK PLACE IN BELGRADE. THE MILITARY RESERVES OF SERBIA WERE CALLED UP FOR A POSSIBLE WAR.

THE SERBIAN GOVERNMENT DEMANDED COMPENSATION FROM AUSTRIA-HUNGARY, CERTAIN THAT RUSSIA, THE SERB'S LONGTIME ALLY, WOULD BACK THEIR CLAIM.

EMPEROR FRANZ JOSEPH MOBILIZED A MILLION AUSTRIAN TROOPS.

"BETTER SAFE THAN SORRY, THIS WAR'S BOUND TO COME SOONER OR LATER."

—COMMENT BY EMPEROR FRANZ JOSEPH TO HIS STAFF

"STOP AGITATING FOR WAR. IT WOULD BE SPLENDID, INDEED VERY TEMPTING, TO CUT THE SERBS TO PIECES, BUT TO ACQUIRE SUCH CHEAP LAURELS COULD RESULT IN A EUROPEAN CONFLAGRATION IN WHICH WE WOULD BE FIGHTING ON TWO FRONTS WITHOUT ANY HOPE OF OVERALL SUCCESS."

—EXCERPT FROM LETTER BY FRANZ FERDINAND TO THE HEAD OF HIS MILITARY CHANCELLERY

BELGRADE SAW THE CREATION OF NARODNA ODBRANA OR "DEFENSE OF THE PEOPLE," AN ORGANIZATION SET UP TO INFLAME THE NATIONAL CONSCIOUSNESS.

"THE NARODNA ODBRANA PROCLAIMS TO THE PEOPLE OF SERBIA THAT AUSTRIA IS OUR FIRST AND GREATEST ENEMY. JUST AS ONCE THE TURKS ATTACKED US FROM THE SOUTH, SO AUSTRIA ATTACKS US TODAY FROM THE NORTH. IF THE NARODNA ODBRANA PREACHES THE NECESSITY OF FIGHTING AUSTRIA, SHE PREACHES THE SACRED TRUTH OF OUR NATIONAL POSITION."

—EXCERPT FROM NARODNA ODBRANA'S MANIFESTO

SMACK

IN THE END, THE WAR WAS AVERTED. GERMANY PUT CONSIDERABLE POLITICAL PRESSURE ON THE CZAR, WHO THEN ANNOUNCED THAT RUSSIA ACCEPTED THE AUSTRIAN ANNEXATION OF BOSNIA-HERZEGOVINA.

SERBIA HAD TO BACK DOWN.
THE CRISIS HAD BLOWN OVER.

VLADIMIR'S SURE THE SECRET POLICE ARE AFTER HIM. HE FLED TO THE SERBIAN BORDER.

SHOULD WE GO INTO HIDING AS WELL?

NAH... THEY DON'T KNOW US.

WE'RE NOBODIES.

VAREŠANIN'S NOT DEAD! THE ASSASSIN MISSED!

KILLED HIMSELF INSTEAD! FIRED THE LAST BULLET INTO HIS OWN MOUTH.

MY COUSIN TOLD ME THAT THE ASSASSIN'S NAME IS BOGDAN ŽERAJIĆ. HE WAS A LAW STUDENT AT THE UNIVERSITY OF ZAGREB.

THEY FOUND A RENDERING OF A GRIMACING MAN HOLDING A SCYTHE IN HIS POCKET.

ŽERAJIĆ! WASN'T HE A FRIEND OF VLADIMIR'S?

THEY WENT TO THE SAME SCHOOL IN MOSTAR.

WHERE IS VLADIMIR? IS HE IN SARAJEVO?

IN VIENNA, I HEARD, HE'S STUDYING ON A SCHOLARSHIP FROM THE SERBIAN GOVERNMENT.

UPON THE CLOSURE OF ITS INVESTIGATION, THE AUSTRIAN POLICE CONCLUDED THAT BOGDAN ŽERAJIĆ WAS A DERANGED INDIVIDUAL, NOT PART OF A CONSPIRACY, AND HAD ACTED ALONE.

HE WAS BURIED IN AN UNMARKED GRAVE IN THE ORTHODOX CEMETERY OF SARAJEVO IN THE SECTION RESERVED FOR CRIMINALS AND SUICIDES.

"EVERYONE KNOWS THE EVIL INFLUENCE OF LAZINESS.
WORK RELIEVES A MAN. BUT THERE IS WORK AND WORK.
THERE IS THE WORK OF THE FREE INDIVIDUAL WHICH MAKES
HIM FEEL A PART OF THE IMMENSE WHOLE. AND THEN THERE
IS THAT OF A SLAVE WHICH DEGRADES."

—PETER KROPOTKIN, ANARCHIST
PHILOSOPHER, 1886

"IF THE BOURGEOISIE REALLY WANTS TO PERFORM
ONE LAST SERVICE FOR HUMANITY; IF ITS LOVE FOR
REAL, COMPLETE WORLDWIDE FREEDOM IS SINCERE;
IF IT WISHES, IN A WORD, TO QUIT BEING REACTIONARY,
THEN THERE IS ONLY ONE THING LEFT FOR IT TO DO:
TO DIE GRACEFULLY, AS QUICKLY AS POSSIBLE."

—MIKHAIL BAKUNIN, ANARCHIST
PHILOSOPHER, 1870

"THE CHASM BETWEEN THE MODERN MILLIONAIRE
WHO SQUANDERS THE PRODUCE OF HUMAN LABOR
IN A GORGEOUS AND VAIN LUXURY, AND THE PAUPER
REDUCED TO A MISERABLE AND INSECURE EXISTENCE,
IS GROWING WIDER AND WIDER, SO AS TO BREAK THE
VERY UNITY OF SOCIETY."

—PETER KROPOTKIN, ANARCHIST
PHILOSOPHER, 1887

THEY WANT THE POOR TO FIGHT THE POOR. THE WAY IT HAS ALWAYS BEEN.

NOT THIS TIME!

THIS TIME, THE POOR FIGHT THEIR REAL ENEMIES!

STOP THINKING ABOUT POLITICS FOR A SECOND AND KISS ME INSTEAD.

GAVRO, DON'T! YOU GET TOO EXCITED.

WHAT ABOUT YOU? DON'T YOU GET EXCITED?

DON'T YOU WANT ME?

I'LL GET EXCITED WHEN WE'RE MARRIED!

YOU LOOK TROUBLED. SOMETHING BOTHERING YOU, GAVRO?

I'VE BEEN THROWN OUT OF SCHOOL BECAUSE OF MY BAD GRADES!

JOVO'S GONNA RIP MY HEAD OFF!

I'M MOVING TO BELGRADE. IF WAR BREAKS OUT, AT LEAST I CAN JOIN THE SERBIAN ARMY.

YOUR DAYS OF GLORY WILL SOON ARRIVE.

THE GOVERNMENT IN SERBIA MIGHT NOT BE PERFECT, BUT AT LEAST THEY'RE NOT THE DAMNED AUSTRIANS!

INDEED!

YOU BOYS SHOULD KEEP YOUR VOICES DOWN!

YOU HAVE NO MONEY. HOW ARE YOU GOING TO GET YOURSELF TO BELGRADE!

WALK!

WALK? IT'S MORE THAN A HUNDRED MILES!

HUNDRED AND TWENTY, ACTUALLY.

YOU SEE, I'VE BEEN THINKING...VLADIMIR SENT ME THIS BOOK, WHAT IS TO BE DONE?.

THERE'S A CHARACTER IN IT, RAKHMETOV, WHO'S A HERMIT AND AN ASCETIC.

HE KEEPS HIMSELF PURE, STRIVING FOR PERFECTION IN PREPARATION FOR THE REVOLUTIONARY FUTURE...

...MAYBE WE SHOULD DO THE SAME!

BECOME HERMITS?

LIVE ASCETICALLY. NO BOOZE. NO SMOKES. NO WOMEN, EVEN!

SOUNDS LIKE A TALL ORDER!

A NECESSARY ONE! I'M STARTING BY WALKING TO BELGRADE. A SOFT LIFE CAN'T PREPARE YOU FOR THE STRENUOUS ORDEAL OF A REVOLUTION!

HMM...

YOU'RE RIGHT. I ADMIRE YOUR DETERMINATION AND WILL DO MY BEST TO FOLLOW YOUR EXAMPLE.

NO DRINK, NO CIGARETTES!

AND NO WOMEN!

TAKE CARE, GAVRO. HAVE A SAFE TRIP!

WILL YOU LOOK AFTER MY BOOKS, WHILE I'M GONE?

CERTAINLY.

BELGRADE

IN 1912, THE SERBIAN CAPITAL WAS FULL OF EXPATRIATE SERBS FROM
BOSNIA AND HERZEGOVNIA, MOST OF THEM STUDENTS AND MOST OF THEM TERRIBLY POOR.

THERE'S RUMORS OF CHRISTIANS IN MACEDONIA BEING SLAUGHTERED BY TURKISH TROOPS. VILLAGES BEING BURNED!

MASS RAPES OF CHRISTIAN WOMEN BY THE MUSLIMS!

MONTENEGRO AND BULGARIA HAVE MADE AN AGREEMENT TO SUPPORT EACH OTHER MILITARILY IN CASE OF WAR.

I'M FROM SARAVEJO. MY DAD OWNS A CAFÉ THERE, A REAL DUMP.

THE AUSTRIANS GAVE HIM THE PERMIT UNDER THE CONDITION THAT HE WORKED FOR THEM AS AN INFORMER, SO NOW HE'S SPYING ON THE GUESTS, HIS FRIENDS, EVERYBODY.

I HATE HIM!

SERBIA AND MONTENEGRO STAND UNITED ON THE QUESTION OF MACEDONIA.

IN BOSNIA, I WAS INVOLVED IN UNION WORK. BECAUSE I PARTICIPATED IN A STRIKE, I WAS BANISHED FROM SARAJEVO, MY HOMETOWN, FOR FIVE YEARS!

THE AUSTRIANS WALKED ME IN HANDCUFFS ALL THE WAY TO TREBINJE. JUST FOR TRYING TO GET A DECENT WAGE I COULD LIVE ON!

AN ULTIMATUM HAS BEEN ISSUED TO TURKEY. PRIME MINISTER NIKOLA PAŠIĆ STATES THAT POLITICAL REFORMS ARE ABSOLUTELY NECESSARY TO PROTECT THE RIGHTS OF ALL CHRISTIANS IN MACEDONIA.

WAR'S COMING!

I WELCOME IT! THE TURKS HAVE OPPRESSED OUR PEOPLE FOR CENTURIES. NOW IT'S THEIR TURN TO SUFFER!

WE'VE HEARD THAT THEY'RE RECRUITING PEOPLE FOR BANDS OF PARTISANS TO SNEAK ACROSS THE BORDER INTO MACEDONIA. WE WANT TO VOLUTEER.

MAJOR TANKOSIĆ'S IN CHARGE OF THE KOMITADJI PARTISAN. I'LL TAKE YOU TO HIS QUARTERS. I WANT TO JOIN MYSELF.

WAIT HERE!

I'LL FIND OUT IF THE MAJOR HAS TIME TO SEE YOU.

FOLKS SAY THAT TANKOSIĆ APPEARS TO BE A GENTL MAN, BUT DON'T LET IT DECEIVE YOU. HE'S A HARSH COMMANDER, READY TO COMMIT ANY ACT TO FULFIL HIS PATRIOTIC DUTY.

DIDN'T HE TAKE PART IN THE MURDER OF THE DESPOT KING ALEXANDER?

GAVRILO PRINCIP!

TAKE YOUR JACKET AND SHIRT OFF, BOY.

DO YOU SUFFER FROM CONSUMPTION?

YES.

PUT YOUR CLOTHES BACK ON.

A KOMITADJI FIGHTS BEHIND ENEMY LINES, HIDES IN THE MOUNTAINS, SLEEPS IN THE RAIN, AND MUST SOMETIMES GO WITHOUT FOOD FOR DAYS.

YOU WOULDN'T LAST LONG UNDER THOSE CIRCUMSTANCES, I'M AFRAID.

YOU... YOU'RE TURNING ME DOWN?

UNFORTUNATELY, YES. BUT DON'T LOSE HEART. THERE'LL BE ANOTHER PLACE FOR YOU TO DO YOUR HEROIC DUTY FOR SERBIA...JUST NOT WITH THE PARTISANS IN MACEDONIA.

ON OCTOBER 8, 1912, MONTENEGRO DECLARED WAR ON TURKEY. TEN DAYS LATER, SERBIA, BULGARIA, AND GREECE FOLLOWED SUIT.

...my life's full of bitterness and gall. I go from nothingness to nothingness and in me, there's less and less of myself left.
Gavro

Dearest Gavro,
Sorry to hear about your rejection, but don't brood too much about it (though I know you probably will!). One's own fate is not easily decrypted and at times we stumble onto our most precious treasures while looking for something else. The important part is to keep your eyes and mind open, should that unexpected opportunity arrive at the door. Don't close yourself off in despair; hope is far too precious to waste on simple disappointment. I miss you and can't wait to see you again.
Love, Jelena

WITHIN A FEW WEEKS, THE TURKS WERE PUSHED ENTIRELY OUT OF CONTINENTAL EUROPE EXCEPT FOR THE AREA SURROUNDING ISTANBUL.

THE TURKS HAVE ABANDONED ALL CLAIMS TO THE BALKAN LANDS AS WELL AS ALL RIGHTS TO CRETE AND THE AEGEAN ISLANDS.

CAN YOU BELIEVE IT? AFTER FIVE HUNDRED YEARS, WE'RE AT LONG LAST FREE OF THEIR RULE.

BUT NOT THANKS TO THE TWO OF US.

I FEEL ASHAMED.

VIENNA, 1913

THE STAFF OFFICE OF ARCHDUKE FRANZ FERDINAND

LET ME GET THIS STRAIGHT: AFTER SERBIA, MONTENEGRO, BULGARIA, AND GREECE DEFEATED TURKEY LAST YEAR, BULGARIA HAS NOW ATTACKED SERBIA AND GREECE?

APPARENTLY THE VICTORS CAN'T AGREE ON HOW TO DIVIDE THE LIBERATED MACEDONIA AMONGST THEMSELVES.

ALSO, ROMANIA HAS ATTACKED BULGARIA...AND SO HAS TURKEY.

AM I THE ONLY ONE CONFUSED HERE?

100

BELGRADE

WHAT THE WARS WITH TURKEY AND BULGARIA HAVE PROVEN IS THAT **ACTION** IS THE ONLY WAY TO CHANGE **ANYTHING!**

IF WE SERBS SHALL LIVE OUT OUR DESTINY, WE MUSTN'T SHY AWAY FROM VIOLENCE.

WE **CAN'T** BE AFRAID OF BECOMING MURDERERS.

BUT, GAVRO, WHAT ABOUT THE RUMORS THAT THE KOMITADJIS KILLED WOMEN AND CHILDREN IN MACEDONIA?

WOMEN AND CHILDREN??!

I DON'T CONDONE THAT, BUT ONE MUST LOOK AT THE **BIGGER** PICTURE HERE.

THINK OF THE SERBS SUFFERING FOR THE LAST FIVE HUNDRED YEARS!

IN THE FACE OF SUCH TREMENDOUS INJUSTICE, WHAT OTHER CHOICE DO WE HAVE BUT TO BECOME **TERRORISTS?**

I MOVED IN WITH A GROUP OF STUDENTS IN AN APARTMENT CLOSE TO THE SCHOOL.

I'M SHARING A ROOM WITH A GUY NAMED TRIFKO GRABEŽ.

WHAT'S HE LIKE?

HAVEN'T MET HIM YET.

...ARREST FOR FOR HITTING A T MY SCHOOL.

THEY EXPELLED ME, BUT IT WAS WORTH IT.

YOU KNOW, I CAME TO BELGRADE LAST YEAR AND IMMEDIATELY NOTICED HOW **FREE** ONE FEELS HERE.

...I CAN STILL SEE THAT OLD FART'S EXPRESSION WHEN I BROKE HIS HUGE HONKER AND TOLD HIM I WAS FED UP WITH HIS SHIT.

TOTALLY DIFFERENT FROM BEING A SERB IN BOSNIA.

AUSTRIAN RULE'S **INTOLE-RABLE!**

COULDN'T AGREE WITH YOU MORE!

GOOD NIGHT, TRIFKO. YOU'RE ALL RIGHT.

GOOD NIGHT.

IF ANARCHISM SHALL SUCCEED AS MORE THAN JUST AN IDEA, HUMAN BEINGS MUST ABANDON **GREED!**

NOT ONLY GREED FOR LAND OR MONEY OR INFLUENCE, BUT ALSO GREED FOR SEXUAL PLEASURES FOR EASY RELIEF.

HOW CAN WE STRIKE FOR FREEDOM FROM OPPRESSION AND FIGHT FOR A JUST SOCIETY IF WE, AT THE SAME TIME, VISIT PROSTITUTES, THE MOST OPPRESSED OF ALL HUMANS?

COME ON, GAVRILO...

...A MAN MUST EAT TO LIVE, AND A MAN MUST EMBRACE A WOMAN NOW AND THEN NOT TO GO CRAZY!

HOW CAN YOU ACCOMPLISH A REVOLUTION, IF ALL THAT'S ON YOUR MIND IS

SEE YOU TOMORROW.

SOMETIMES I FEAR THAT NEDELJKO'S A BLOODY SOCIALIST!

1914

I WANNA TALK TO YOU ABOUT SOMETHING.

YEAH?

NOT HERE.

SO? LET'S HEAR IT.

THIS IS FROM A GERMAN NEWSPAPER.

WHEN I READ IT, I SUDDENLY FELT MY DESTINY REVEAL ITSELF TO ME IN ALL ITS GLORY.

ARCHDUKE FRANZ FERDINAND'S COMING TO SARAJEVO.

WE MUST ASSASSINATE HIM!

WOULDN'T IT BE BETTER TO KILL THE AUSTRIAN GOVERNOR?

POTIOREK'S NOTHING BUT A HIRED HAND. ASSASSINATING THE HEIR WOULD STRIKE AT THE VERY HEART OF THE MONARCHY.

I'M IN.

THE HEIR WILL BE GUARDED BY SOLDIERS AND PLAINCLOTHES POLICE. NO CHANCE OF GETTING TO HIM WITH THE KNIFE.

TRUE.

WE'LL NEED GUNS, PERHAPS BOMBS.

WHICH WE CAN BUY IN THE ARMY SUPPLY STORE RIGHT DOWN THE STREET.

WITH WHAT MONEY?

CIGO, WE'RE DETERMINED TO ASSASSINATE ARCHDUKE FRANZ FERDINAND.

♪

YOU WERE WITH THE KOMITADJIS DURING THE WAR. COULD YOU GET SOME WEAPONS FROM THEM FOR OUR ENDEAVOR?

I KNOW THEY PROCURE ARMS FROM THE GUERRILLA OPERATIONS IN GREEK MACEDONIA.

LET ME TALK TO SOMEONE.

THAT'S OUR HIGHEST ASPIRATION!

HAVE YOU EVER KILLED ANYBODY BEFORE?

I'M MERELY A STUDENT, SIR, AND HAVEN'T HAD THE OPPORTUNITY, BUT I CAN ASSURE YOU, THAT I WON'T HESITATE IN THE FACE OF GLORY.

AND ARE YOU WILLING TO DIE YOURSELF IN THE ATTEMPT?

NOTHING WOULD MAKE ME HAPPIER THAN TO GIVE MY LIFE FOR MY BELOVED HOMELAND.

EVER HEARD OF THE TERROR ORGANIZATION UNIFICATION OR DEATH? SOME PEOPLE ALSO REFER TO IT AS THE BLACK HAND?

CERTAINLY. IT'S FAMOUS.

TANKOSIĆ WILL PROVIDE US WITH GUNS AND BOMBS, NO PROBLEM.

HE'LL ALSO GIVE US ACCESS TO THE SECRET NETWORK THAT CAN SMUGGLE US ACROSS THE BORDER AND THROUGH BOSNIA TO SARAJEVO.

WE DON'T WANT TO BE STOPPED BY AUSTRIAN PATROLS.

CIGO TOLD ME THAT TANKOSIĆ'S THE NUMBER TWO MAN IN THE BLACK HAND, JUST BELOW THE LEGENDARY APIS.

TANKOSIĆ SAYS WE HAVE TO JOIN.

FANTASTIC!

I, IN JOINING UNIFICATION OR DEATH, SWEAR BY THE SUN THAT WARMS ME, BY THE EARTH THAT NOURISHES ME, BEFORE GOD, BY THE BLOOD OF OUR ANCESTORS, ON MY HONOR, AND ON MY LIFE, THAT I'LL FROM THIS MOMENT UNTIL MY DEATH BE FAITHFUL TO THE LAWS OF THIS ORGANIZATION, AND THAT I'LL ALWAYS BE READY TO MAKE ANY SACRIFICE FOR IT.

I SWEAR BEFORE GOD, ON MY HONOR AND MY LIFE, THAT I'LL TAKE ALL SECRETS ABOUT THIS ORGANIZATION INTO MY GRAVE WITH ME.

TAKE THESE BOYS OUT TO THE WOODS AND TEACH THEM HOW TO SHOOT.

I GOT YOUR STUFF.

FOUR BROWNINGS, LOADED WITH SEVEN SHOTS EACH, FOUR EXTRA MAGAZINES, ALSO LOADED, AND SIX BOMBS.

THE BOMBS ARE EASY TO OPERATE. JUST UNSCREW THE SAFETY CAP, KNOCK THE BOMB AGAINST SOMETHING HARD, AND IT'LL EXPLODE TEN SECONDS LATER.

MAKE SURE YOU'RE NOT CAUGHT, EVEN BY THE SERBIAN POLICE, WITH THESE WEAPONS ON YOU.

WE KNOW.

TOMORROW YOU'LL BOARD THE STEAMER TO ŠABAC.

ONCE YOU GET THERE, FIND CAPTAIN POPOVIĆ OF THE FRONTIER GENDARMERIE AND GIVE HIM THIS CARD WITH MY INITIALS ON IT. HE'LL GET YOU SMUGGLED INTO BOSNIA.

HERE'S SOME MONEY FOR THE TRIP.

BUT THIS IS TOTALLY INADEQUATE!

IT'S ALL I CAN GIVE YOU.

IMPROVISE, THAT'S WHAT I USED TO DO WITH THE KOMITADJIS IN THE MACEDONAN MOUNTAINS.

ONE MORE THING: NONE OF YOU CAN BE TAKEN ALIVE BY THE AUSTRIANS AFTER YOU KILL THE ARCHDUKE.

HERE'S A PACKAGE OF CYANIDE FOR EACH OF YOU. SWALLOW IT AFTER YOUR GLORIOUS DEED.

EITHER THIS OR CONSUMPTION, WHAT'S THE DIFFERENCE.

AS BOGDAN ŽERAJIĆ WROTE: "HE WHO WANTS TO LIVE, HAS TO DIE. HE WHO IS READY TO DIE, WILL LIVE FOREVER."

LONG LIVE SERBIA!

LONG LIVE SERBIA!

114

IF YOU EVER COME BACK HERE, WE'LL REALLY WORK YOU OVER!

WHAT HAPPENED?

YOUR BUDDY TRIFKO CHEATS AT CARDS!

BLOODY BOSNIAN RIFFRAFF!

I CAN LIVE WITH THE SCORN OF THE AUSTRIANS, BUT IT BREAKS MY HEART TO FEEL IT FROM OUR OWN PEOPLE, FROM SERBIANS!

MAYBE YOU SHOULDN'T CHEAT THEN.

I DON'T CHEAT!

I JUST STEAL AND LIE!

A MUTUAL FRIEND TOLD ME TO GIVE YOU THIS. WE NEED TO CROSS THE DRINA INTO BOSNIA. SECRETLY.

TAKE THE TRAIN DOWN TO LOZNICA AND SHOW THIS NOTE TO CAPTAIN PRVANOVIČ IN THE GENDARMERIE THERE. HE'LL TAKE YOU ACROSS WHERE HE THINKS BEST.

THE TRAIN? WE HAVE VERY LITTLE MONEY.

I'LL MAKE A WARRANT STATING THAT YOU'RE CUSTOMS OFFICIALS. IT'LL GIVE YOU A SUBSTANTIAL REDUCTION ON THE TICKET PRICES.

ACROSS THE BORDER IN BOSNIA

CAPTAIN! A DISPATCH FROM GOVERNOR POTIOREK HIMSELF.

APPARENTLY, AN ASSASSIN IS TRYING TO CROSS THE BORDER. GIVE INSTRUCTIONS TO THE BORDER GUARDS TO CHECK ALL PAPERS MORE CAREFULLY. AND SEND OUT EXTRA PATROLS AT NIGHT.

YES, SIR!

CATCHING THIS GUY JUST MIGHT GET ME OUT OF THIS HELLHOLE AND BACK TO SALZBURG.

123

I HAD A NIGHTMARE LAST NIGHT.

YEAH?

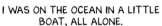

I WAS ON THE OCEAN IN A LITTLE BOAT, ALL ALONE.

IT WAS DARK, IN THE MIDDLE OF THE NIGHT, AND A FIERCE WIND WAS BLOWING.

I KEPT HEARING OUR CHILDREN CALLING FOR HELP, SHOUTING THAT THEY WERE DROWNING, BUT I COULDN'T SEE THEM.

SO I JUMPED INTO THE BLACK WATER. IT WAS TERRIBLY COLD.

LIKE ICE.

I WENT DOWN FAST.

LARGE FISH SWAM BY ME.

I COULD FEEL THEIR SLIMY BODIES AGAINST MY SKIN.

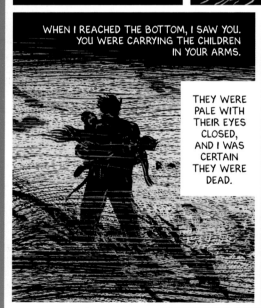

WHEN I REACHED THE BOTTOM, I SAW YOU. YOU WERE CARRYING THE CHILDREN IN YOUR ARMS.

THEY WERE PALE WITH THEIR EYES CLOSED, AND I WAS CERTAIN THEY WERE DEAD.

AN INCREDIBLE SADNESS OVERWHELMED ME. BUT YOU SMILED AND SAID "DON'T WORRY, THEY'RE ONLY SLEEPING."

AND HOLDING OUT MY HAND, YOU LED US ALL OUT OF THE WATER AND TO THE SAFETY OF THE SHORE.

DAWN HAD BROKE AS WE WALKED UP UNTO THE BEACH, AND THE CHILDREN WOKE UP. ERNST WAS INSTANTLY HUNGRY THE WAY HE ALWAYS IS IN THE MORNING.

YOU DON'T NEED TO WORRY ABOUT ME, DEAR. I BEAT THE TUBERCULOSIS SIXTEEN YEARS AGO, AND THE ASTHMA ISN'T REALLY BOTHERING ME THESE DAYS.

I KNOW.

I THANK GOD FOR HIS SMALL MERCIES EVERY DAY.

128

DISPATCHES FROM SARAJEVO REPORT OF A SERBIAN ASSASSIN TRYING TO CROSS THE BORDER INTO BOSNIA! BE EVEN MORE VIGILANT THAN USUAL, SERGEANT!

YESSIR!

IT'S GONNA RAIN.

AND THE CAPTAIN'S SITTING ON HIS FAT ASS INSIDE, DRY AS A NUN'S CUNT!

QUIET!

WE'RE GOING TO DO THIS THING... KILL OURSELVES AFTERWARDS...

...I'M RECONCILED WITH THAT, AT PEACE WITH BOTH THE DEED AND MY OWN DEATH, BUT...

A GIRL I WAS SEEING IN BELGRADE, ANA, BEGGED ME NOT TO GO. NOT THAT SHE KNEW ANYTHING ABOUT OUR PLAN, BUT SHE MUST HAVE SENSED SOMETHING IN MY DEMEANOR...I...

WELL, SHE SAID SHE LOVED ME.

AND YOU? HOW DO YOU FEEL ABOUT HER?

HOW DO YOU KNOW THAT YOU LOVE SOMEBODY, GAVRO?

WHEN, FOR ONCE, YOUR OWN SELF IS NOT THE MOST IMPORTANT THING IN THE WORLD.

RRRAAA

MAYBE WE SHOULDN'T WORRY SO MUCH ABOUT CATCHING OUR DEATH!

BETTER TO DIE IN ACCOMPLISHING SOMETHING THAN TO LIVE LIKE MY FAMILY...LIKE ALL OF THE PEOPLE OF MY VALLEY, ACTUALLY...

...BEATEN DOWN, BROKEN BY LIFE, SEEING YOUR CHILDREN PERISH ONE BY ONE FROM LACK OF PROPER CARE AND NOURISHMENT, WHILE THE LANDLORDS—MUSLIM OR AUSTRIAN, WHAT'S THE DIFFERENCE?—TAKE A POUND OF YOUR FLESH EVERY YEAR!

WE'RE NOT ONLY KILLING THE HEIR FOR JUSTICE BUT ALSO FOR **REVENGE!**

IS THAT REALLY ALL WE'RE AFTER?

THAT AND **POWER.**

NO...

...AT LEAST NOT FOR ME. I'M DOING IT FOR SOMETHING ELSE, SOMETHING MUCH LESS TANGIBLE. NOT HARMONY, OF COURSE, AND NOT PEACE...BUT... I GUESS I JUST WISH EVERYBODY ON EARTH TO BE ABLE TO SLEEP PEACEFULLY AT NIGHT.

ARE WE GONNA ACCOMPLISH THAT THROUGH MURDER?

NO REAL CHANGE EVER HAPPENED WITHOUT BLOODSHED. YOU KNOW THAT!

THAT'S TRUE... BUT TONIGHT I WISH IT WAS A LIE!

138

SARAJEVO CITY HALL

MY DEAR GOVERNOR, YOU MUST BE SENSITIVE TO THE FACT THAT IT COULD CREATE A LOT OF RESENTMENT TO RENAME OUR MAIN THOROUGHFARE "FRANZ FERDINAND STREET" JUST BECAUSE THE HEIR COMES TO TOWN ON AN OFFICIAL VISIT.

I DIDN'T COME HERE FOR YOUR OPINION, MR. MAYOR, BUT TO GIVE YOU AN INSTRUCTION.

GET IT DONE! AND MAKE SURE A LOT OF YOUR CITIZENS ARE OUT ON THE STREETS, SHOWING THE ARCHDUKE THEIR GRATITUDE, DEVOTION, AND LOYALTY.

OF COURSE.

I'M GLAD YOU ALL AGREED TO COME.

ANOTHER TEAM OF ASSASSINS ARE ENTERING TOWN TOMORROW.

I'VE BEEN GIVEN WORD THAT THE WEAPONS ARE WAITING FOR US IN TUZLA.

EVERYTHING'S READY.

WHO WILL BRING THE ARMS INTO SARAJEVO?

ME.

144

147

THE AUSTRIANS
DECIDE
EVERYTHING!

WHERE YOU CAN LIVE,
IF YOU CAN WORK,
WHETHER OR NOT YOU'RE
ALLOWED TO TRAVEL.

AT LEAST I CAN
DECIDE WHEN
TO DIE!

I KNOW IT'S A SIN TO KILL, BUT STILL...

I HAVE TO DO THIS THING THAT WE PLAN, TO PAY THE AUSTRIANS BACK! PAY THEM BACK FOR EVERY TIME ONE OF THEM GAVE ME THAT LOOK OF SUPERIORITY. PAY THEM BACK FOR EVERY SERB THAT'S BEEN TREATED LIKE A DOG BY THEM.

ALL THE SCORN, ALL THE HUMILIATION JUST PENTS UP INSIDE YOU, PUTS A STRANGLEHOLD ON YOUR WHOLE BEING. SUFFOCATES YOU!

BUILDS UP IN YOUR HEART, BECOMES TOO MUCH TO BEAR.

YOU SHOULD PUT SOME OF THIS KINDA TALK INTO YOUR POETRY INSTEAD OF ALL THAT SAPPY STUFF ABOUT GIRLS.

IT'S BAD LUCK TO WRITE POEMS ABOUT MURDER.

I HAVE NEVER TOLD ANYBODY THIS, BUT I SOMETIMES CONSIDER KILLING MYSELF.

ISN'T IT BETTER TO KILL YOUR OPPRESSOR INSTEAD?

IT'S A MISERY EITHER WAY.

ACCORDING TO THE NEWSPAPERS, THE ARCHDUKE WILL BE STAYING AT THE ILIDŽE SPA HOTEL OUTSIDE TOWN.

THROW THE BOMBS AT THE CAR, WHEN IT PASSES BY.

HE'LL BE TOO CLOSELY GUARDED THERE. SOLDIERS EVERYWHERE. OUR BEST CHANCE IS HERE IN SARAJEVO, WHERE WE CAN HIDE IN THE CROWDS.

OR GET HIM WITH THE GUN.

AS SOON AS THE ROUTE'S PUBLISHED, I'LL DETERMINE THE POSITIONS OF OUR TWO TEAMS.

SHOULDN'T YOU TELL US WHO THE OTHER THREE GUNMEN ARE?

PROBABLY SAFER IF YOU DON'T KNOW EACH OTHER'S IDENTITY TILL THE DAY BEFORE THE DEED, JUST IN CASE.

JUST IN CASE.

I WENT OVER THE ITINERARY OF HIS HIGHNESS AND COULDN'T HELP BUT NOTICE THAT THE VISIT TO SARAJEVO FALLS ON ST. VITUS' DAY, THE ONE THE SERBS REFER TO AS VIDOVDAN.

SO?

THE ILIDŽE SPA HOTEL

HOW WAS YOUR HUNT TODAY, YOUR HIGHNESS?

FINE, ALTHOUGH RATHER HOT.

DID YOU KNOW THAT IN THE COURSE OF MY HUNTING CAREER SO FAR, I'VE KILLED MORE THAN A QUARTER OF A MILLION HEAD OF GAME, AMONG THEM SIX THOUSAND STAGS?

IMPRESSIVE.

FANTASTIC!

MAY I AGAIN IMPLORE YOUR HIGHNESS TO PLEASE RECONSIDER THE VISIT TO SARAJEVO? THE PLACE'S A HOTBED OF RADICALS. I FEAR FOR THE LIFE OF MY BELOVED ARCHDUKE. WHY NOT CANCEL AND GO BACK TO VIENNA TOMORROW?

PERHAPS I SHOULD. THE PROSPECT OF SWEATING AROUND THE CITY ALL DAY IN FULL UNIFORM SEEMS DECIDEDLY UNAPPEALING.

I THINK IT UNWISE OF YOUR HIGHNESS TO CUT THE TRIP SHORT AT THIS POINT.

THE CROATS EXPECT A VISIT FROM YOU AFTER SARAJEVO.

IT'S IMPERATIVE THAT THE DOUBLE MONARCHY RETAIN THEIR LOYALTY.

GOOD POINT. SARAJEVO IT IS THEN!

DANILO?

I'VE BEEN WAITING FOR YOU.

GAVRO, WE MUST CALL OFF THE ASSASSINATION!

NEVER!

FORGET THE AUSTRIAN OPPRESSION, FORGET YOUR OWN GLORY, AND THINK OF OUR PEOPLE!

THE KILLING OF THE HEIR COULD BRING HORRIBLE REPRISALS FROM VIENNA, PERHAPS EVEN WAR!

A WAR SERBIA WOULD WIN!

THERE'S NO GUARANTEE OF THAT.

DANILO, MY FRIEND, OUR PEOPLE HAVE SUFFERED BLOODSUCKING, CRUEL LANDLORDS FOR FIVE HUNDRED YEARS.

NOW, WE HAVE SENT THE TURKS BACK TO ISTANBUL, BRINGING NO OTHER RICHES THAN THEIR OWN DEAD.

THE TIME HAS COME FOR THE AUSTRIANS TO LEAVE.

THROUGH VIOLENCE, THROUGH PURE TERROR, WE'LL MAKE THEM UNDERSTAND THAT THEIR PRESENCE HERE IS JUST TOO DEAR COMPARED TO THE LITTLE THEY CAN SQUEEZE OUT OF OUR IMPOVERISHED PEOPLE!

THE FIRST PRICE THE OPPRESSORS PAY IS THE LIFE OF THE HEIR TO THE EMPEROR'S THRONE.

WE'VE ENDURED ENOUGH AND CAN AT LONG LAST HOPE FOR A BRIGHTER FUTURE FOR OUR PEOPLE!

THAT'S THE TRUTH, DANILO!

IT MIGHT BE WRITTEN IN WATER, BUT WHAT ELSE HAVE WE GOT?

Many people I have loved dearly are dead. My grandfather's passing especially pained me and still causes me grief. But even though he is long gone, he lives in me, as I believe. I lived in him, when he was alive.

That is all we are, a chain of hands holding each other through time, nothing more but certainly nothing less, and the beauty of that will never be erased even when my little lantern is put out.

UPON THE ARRIVAL OF THE ARCHDUKE'S CAR AT THE GOVERNOR'S RESIDENCE, SOPHIE WAS FOUND TO BE DEAD. FRANZ FERDINAND PERISHED A FEW MINUTES LATER.

AUSTRIAN POLICE SOON FOUND OUT THAT GAVRILO PRINCIP HAD STAYED WITH DANILO ILIĆ IN THE TIME LEADING UP TO THE ASSASSINATION.

DURING INTERROGATION, ILIĆ ADMITTED TO BEING PART OF THE PLOT TO ASSASSINATE FRANZ FERDINAND AND NOT ONLY GAVE THE POLICE THE NAMES OF TRIFKO GRABEŽ, MUHAMED MEHMEDBAŠIĆ, CVJETKO POPOVIĆ, THE ČUBRILOVIĆ BROTHERS, AND MIŠKO JOVANOVIĆ BUT ALSO REVEALED THE CONNECTION TO THE BLACK HAND.

ALL THE CONSPIRATORS WERE ARRESTED, EXCEPT MUHAMED MEHMEDBAŠIĆ, WHO MANAGED TO ESCAPE TO MONTENEGRO.

ON JULY 23, AUSTRIA-HUNGARY POSED AN ULTIMATUM FULL
OF UNREASONABLE DEMANDS TO SERBIA.

THE GOVERNMENT IN BELGRADE TRIED TO ACCOMMODATE EMPEROR FRANZ JOSEPH
AS BEST IT COULD WITHOUT LOSING FACE BUT TO NO AVAIL.

AUSTRIA-HUNGARY DECLARED
WAR ON SERBIA ON JULY 28.

THE CZAR IMMEDIATELY SIGNED AN ORDER FOR GENERAL MOBILIZATION OF THE RUSSIAN ARMY.

GERMANY DEMANDED THAT RUSSIA STAND DOWN, AND WHEN THE
CHALLENGE WAS IGNORED, GERMANY DECLARED WAR ON RUSSIA.

TWO DAYS LATER, THE GERMANS ALSO DECLARED WAR ON FRANCE, AND THE GERMAN ARMY ENTERED
FRENCH SOIL THROUGH BELGIUM.

THE VIOLATION OF NEUTRAL BELGIUM COMPELLED BRITAIN TO DECLARE WAR ON GERMANY.

"THE LIGHTS ARE GOING OUT ALL OVER EUROPE. WE
SHALL NOT SEE THEM LIT AGAIN IN OUR LIFETIME."

—SIR EDWARD GREY, FOREIGN
SECRETARY OF GREAT BRITAIN,
AUGUST 3, 1914

GAVRILO PRINCIP, NEDELJKO ČABRINOVIĆ, AND TRIFKO GRABEŽ WERE UNDER TWENTY ON JUNE 28, 1914 AND NOT ELIGIBLE FOR THE DEATH PENALTY UNDER AUSTRIAN LAW. THEY EACH RECEIVED TWENTY-YEAR PRISON SENTENCES.

ČABRINOVIĆ DIED OF TUBERCULOSIS IN JANUARY 1916.

GRABEŽ SUCCUMBED TO THE SAME DISEASE IN FEBRUARY 1918.

DANILO ILIĆ, MIŠKO JOVANOVIĆ, AND VELJKO ČUBRILOVIĆ ALL RECEIVED DEATH SENTENCES AND WERE EXECUTED IN SARAJEVO WITHOUT INCIDENT ON FEBRUARY 3, 1915.

VASO ČUBRILOVIĆ WAS SENTENCED TO SIXTEEN YEARS IN PRISON BUT RELEASED BY THE ALLIES AFTER THE WAR. HE BECAME A UNIVERSITY PROFESSOR AND LATER SERVED AS YUGOSLAVIA'S MINISTER OF FORESTS.

CVJETKO POPOVIĆ WAS SENTENCED TO THIRTEEN YEARS IN PRISON AND ALSO RELEASED BY THE ALLIES. HE BECAME THE CURATOR OF THE ETHNOGRAPHIC DEPARTMENT OF THE SARAJEVO MUSEUM.

MUHAMED MEHMEDBAŠIĆ RETURNED TO SARAJEVO AFTER THE WAR AND WAS PARDONED FOR HIS ROLE IN THE ASSASSINATION. HE DIED DURING WORLD WAR II.

SERBIA EVENTUALLY
SUFFERED MILITARY DEFEAT
BY THE AUSTRIANS. THE
BLACK HAND WAS BLAMED
FOR IGNITING THE WAR.
APIS WAS ARRESTED AND
EXECUTED ON JUNE 11, 1913.

VOJA TANKOSIĆ SERVED IN THE SERBIAN ARMY AND WAS KILLED IN ACTION IN 1915.

VLADIMIR GAČINOVIĆ DIED UNDER MYSTERIOUS CIRCUMSTANCES, ALSO IN 1917, POSSIBLY POISONED BY EITHER AUSTRIAN SPIES OR THE SERBIAN SECRET POLICE.

MILAN CIGANOVIĆ SPENT THE WAR YEARS IN THE UNITED STATES. HE RETURNED TO SERBIA IN 1919, MARRIED, AND SETTLED DOWN AS A FARMER. CIGANOVIĆ DIED IN 1927.

EMPEROR FRANZ JOSEPH PASSED AWAY ON NOVEMBER 21, 1916, AND WAS SUCCEEDED BY HIS GREAT-NEPHEW KARL.

OSKAR POTIOREK LED THE UNSUCCESSFUL FIRST AUSTRIAN INVASION OF SERBIA AND WAS FORCED INTO RETIREMENT AFTERWARDS. HE DIED IN 1933.

JELENA MILIŠIĆ SURVIVED THE WAR AND BECAME A TEACHER AT SARAJEVO'S ACADEMIC HIGH SCHOOL.

SHE SELDOM SPOKE OF HER RELATIONSHIP WITH GAVRILO PRINCIP.

ON APRIL 28, 1918, GAVRILO PRINCIP DIED IN THE TEREZIN PRISON CAMP, PARTLY OF TUBERCULOSIS, PARTLY OF MALTREATMENT.

HE WEIGHED EIGHTY-EIGHT POUNDS.

ON THE WALL OF HIS CELL, HE'D SCRIBBLED A POEM:

"OUR GHOSTS WILL WALK
THROUGH VIENNA,
AND ROAM THE PALACE,
FRIGHTENING THE LORDS."

GAVRILO'S REMAINS WERE EVENTUALLY BURIED IN THE ORTHODOX CEMETARY IN SARAJEVO.

ABOUT 15,000,000
HUMAN BEINGS WERE
KILLED IN THE GREAT
WAR, AMONG THEM
1,260,000 SERBS,
28 PERCENT OF
SERBIA'S POPULATION.

AFTER THE WAR, GAVRILO WAS HAILED AS THE HERO OF THE NEWLY FORMED STATE OF YUGOSLAVIA, WHICH INCLUDED SERBIA AND BOSNIA-HERZEGOVINA. HE WAS REVERED AS THE "ANNUNCIATOR OF LIBERTY" FOR INSTIGATING THE RELEASE FROM AUSTRIAN YOKE.

AS A CELEBRATION OF HIS DEED, TWO EMBOSSED FOOTPRINTS WERE PLACED ON THE SPOT OF THE SIDEWALK IN FRONT OF SCHILLER'S DELICATESSEN FROM WHERE GAVRILO FIRED THE FATAL SHOTS AT FRANZ FERDINAND AND SOPHIE.

AFTER THE COLLAPSE OF YUGOSLAVIA IN THE EARLY 1990S, THE FOOTPRINTS WERE REMOVED. THEY WERE NOT PRESENT ON MAY 27, 1992, THE DAY OF THE SO-CALLED "BREADLINE MASSACRE," WHEN SERBIAN MILITARY FORCES SHELLED THE MARKET IN SARAJEVO, LOCATED JUST A FEW BLOCKS AWAY.

"I'M A YUGOSLAV NATIONALIST, AND I BELIEVE IN THE UNIFICATION OF ALL SOUTHERN SLAVS, FREE OF AUSTRIAN RULE. I TRIED TO REALIZE THAT GOAL BY MEANS OF TERROR.

"I'M NOT A CRIMINAL, BECAUSE I DESTROYED THAT WHICH WAS EVIL. I THINK THAT I'M GOOD.

"THE IDEA GREW IN US, SO WE CARRIED OUT THE ASSASSINATION.

"WE LOVED OUR PEOPLE.

"WE LOVED OUR PEOPLE!"

"I DON'T WANT TO SAY ANYTHING ELSE IN MY DEFENSE."

COURT TRANSCRIPT OF STATEMENTS BY GAVRILO PRINCIP, SARAJEVO, OCTOBER 23, 1914

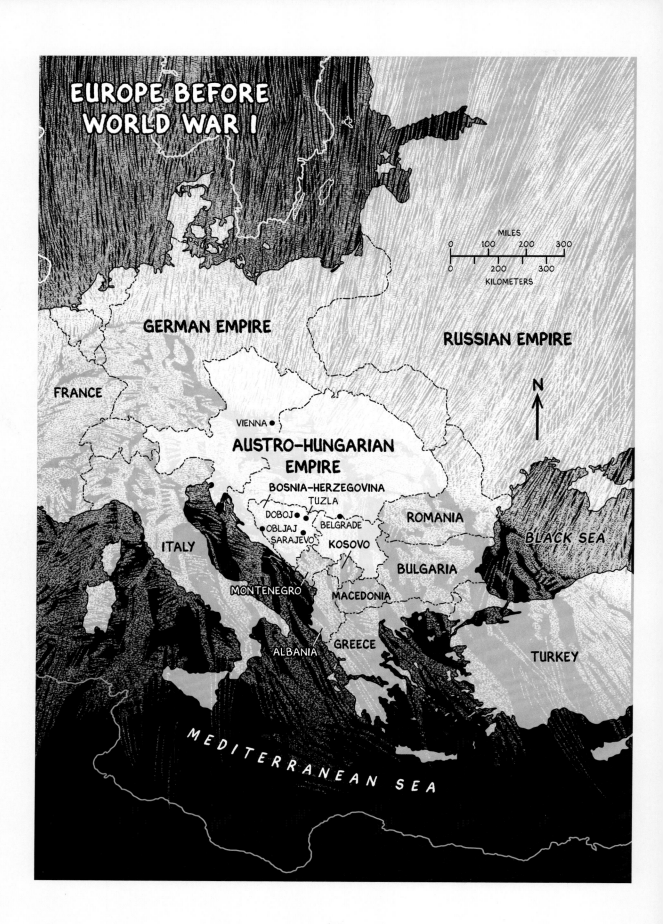

EUROPE BEFORE WORLD WAR I

GERMAN EMPIRE

RUSSIAN EMPIRE

FRANCE

MILES
0 100 200 300
0 200 300
KILOMETERS

N

VIENNA •

AUSTRO-HUNGARIAN EMPIRE

BOSNIA-HERZEGOVINA

TUZLA

DOBOJ •

OBLJAJ •

SARAJEVO

BELGRADE •

KOSOVO

ROMANIA

BLACK SEA

ITALY

BULGARIA

MONTENEGRO

MACEDONIA

ALBANIA

GREECE

TURKEY

MEDITERRANEAN SEA

AFTERWORD

Can a single individual make a difference in the course of the history of the world? Karl Marx, with his theory of historical inevitability, would certainly say no. I think that Gavrilo Princip, being a follower of Marx, would have agreed with his idol. As for myself, I'm not so sure.

The inspiration for this book is due, in no small measure, to the sixteen-volume Grimberg's *Verdenshistorie* (*History of the World* by Carl Grimberg). I came across those books on my grandmother's bookshelf, and perusing these books as a child introduced me to the famous shot in Sarajevo that ignited World War I. While at the dentist about nine years ago, I read an article that focused on the famous sandwich of Gavrilo Princip. According to the article, Princip had given up on assassinating Franz Ferdinand and went to buy something to eat. Only by happenstance did he end up with the opportunity to shoot the archduke. It's amazing how coincidences and incompetence actually made the assassination on that summer day in 1914 possible. The fact that Princip and his friends saw themselves as terrorists and were very proud of it also caught my attention. I live in New York City, a block and a half from where the World Trade Center used to stand. I experienced the terrorist attacks of September 11, 2001, firsthand. The parallels between that event and one in Sarajevo eighty-seven years earlier were striking to me. A small number of people of limited means carried out an act with broad repercussions. I felt that this idea might work well as a graphic novel and that perhaps making it could help me better understand what drives people to become terrorists.

With my curiosity stoked, I went on to investigate the subject. I spent many days at the New York Public Library in the Stephen A. Schwarzman Building on Fifth Avenue and 42nd Street in New York City. I have fond memories of the friendly staff, who went deep into the library vaults to find old, old books, which I studied in the gorgeous reading room. As I learned more about the political situation in the Balkans leading up to World War I and about the history of the region, I felt, to my surprise, a good deal of sympathy for the Serbs. During the Balkan War in the 1990s, which included genocide and the infamous shelling of Sarajevo, the Serbs had gained a horrid reputation. Without condoning those atrocities, one could, with the history of the Serbs in mind, at least get a glimmer of understanding for their ferocity. I also somewhat changed my view of Gavrilo Princip and Franz Ferdinand. Although neither of them were innocent, their motivations and actions were understandable. Empathy for both the murderer and his victim came easily to me. And so I decided to write this book.

I knew from the outset that I would not make a history book but rather a graphic novel more in the vein of a docudrama. Certain liberties had to be taken for the story to work. I put words in the mouths of my characters that I did not necessarily have historical sources for, but I did my best to stay true to my understanding of the people I attempted to bring to life. There is nothing in the book that I know to be historically false, but there is a lot that came from my own imagination. Just as I believe Gavrilo was used by certain elements in Serbia, who wanted to foment a war with Austria, I have used him for my own narrative and artistic purposes. I hope he can forgive me for that.

I was a young man in Europe in the early 1980s during one of the tenser periods of the Cold War. My friends and I were sure we would never reach old age. We took it as a given that we would all perish in the nuclear holocaust that seemed inevitable to us. We were wrong. A crisis that would compel either of the superpowers over the brink to press the dreaded nuclear missile button just never occurred. Instead the Soviet Union collapsed, and although the world is by no means a safe place, it is at least still around. Luckily, the Cold War never had its Gavrilo Princip.

Henrik Rehr
August 2014

ABOUT THE AUTHOR

Henrik Rehr was born in 1964 in Odense, Denmark. His first graphic novel, *Drømmen om langskibene (The Dream of the Longships)*, was published in 1987, and he has subsequently created twenty-four more graphic novels, among them *Tribeca Sunset*, concerning the 9/11 terrorist attack on the World Trade Center. From 1989 to 2006, he drew the syndicated newspaper comic strip *Ferd'nand*, and from 2001 to 2003 he created another strip, *Sandslotte (Castles in the Sand)*. Rehr has also worked as an artist on *Rasmus Klump (Petzi)* and *Beetle Bailey*. He moved from his native Denmark to the United States in 1992 and lives in downtown Manhattan with his wife and two sons.